FEB 2 9 2000

HURRICANE!

by Corinne Demas

illustrations by Lenice U. Strohmeier

MARSHALL CAVENDISH   NEW YORK

Marshall Cavendish, 99 White Plains Road, Tarrytown, NY 10591

Library of Congress Cataloging-in-Publication Data
Hurricane! / by Corinne Demas ; illustrations by Lenice U. Strohmeier.
p. cm.
Summary: Margo and her family prepare for and experience Hurricane Bob, which makes the
electricity go out for five days, but leaves their house intact.
ISBN 0-7614-5052-1
[1. Hurricane Bob, 1991–Fiction. 2. Hurricanes–Fiction.] I. Strohmeier, Lenice U., ill. II. Title.
PZ7.B61917Hu   1999   [Fic]–dc21   98-46891   CIP   AC

The text of this book is set in 14 point Goudy Old Style.
The illustrations are rendered in watercolors.
Printed in Hong Kong
First edition
1 3 5 6 4 2

For Daddy,
who played his harmonica through the worst of storms.
—C. D.

In memory of my mother,
Janice Z. Ulan.
—L. U. S.

Hurricane Bob is coming! We have only a few hours to get ready before it hits our coast.

Daddy rushes to bring in the outdoor table and chairs and the striped umbrella. I grab the clothes from the clothes line. Our dog, Pepper, catches an undershirt that flies away in the growing wind.

Mommy fills every Thermos and jug and pot and pail with water. If the hurricane knocks out the power, we won't be able to get water, because our well has an electric pump.

"Fill up the bathtub, Margo," Mommy tells me. I dash upstairs to the bathroom and fill up the tub to the very top.

Then I run out to the vegetable garden with my basket and pick all the lettuce and beans and tomatoes, even the ones that aren't ripe yet. I zip through the flower garden and cut all the roses and phlox and the lilies that are as tall as I am. Mommy fills all our vases with flowers, and it looks like our garden has come indoors.

Our little boat, *Allegro*, is anchored in the bay. I drive down to the harbor with Daddy. I watch from shore while he brings *Allegro* in to the pier. She bounces up and down in the waves. I help him tie her to the dock.

"She's secure now," Daddy says.

The sky and the sea are the same gray. You can't tell where the water ends in the distance and the sky begins. The wind is so strong I can lean against it without falling down.

Families who live near the water are nailing plywood over their windows. They're going to take shelter in the school on the hill. I sort of wish we had to go there, too.

We tape an X on our big window to keep the glass in place.

"Just in case," Daddy says.

It's lunchtime, but Hurricane Bob still hasn't come. I keep watching for it.

"Eat your sandwich," says Mommy.

The weather radio tells us that Bob has already hit the islands not far away. It's sweeping across the land and sea.

"When will it get here?" I ask.

"Any time now," Mommy says.

Pepper can tell the hurricane is coming. He keeps circling on his mat. I bring him all his dog toys and chews, but he is still too nervous to settle down.

"What about the wild animals?" I ask.

"They've all found safe places to hide till the hurricane passes over," Mommy says.

After lunch we start a jigsaw puzzle on the dining table. There are a thousand pieces. I try to look for the corners and edges. The wind is getting stronger and louder.

The sky is dark. The bayberry bushes start whipping around. The pine trees sway one way, then the other. My swing looks like I'm sailing back and forth on it, higher and higher, but no one is sitting on it at all.

I cuddle with Mommy and Daddy on the sofa in the corner. Because this is a special time, we let Pepper up on the sofa with us, too.

"Will our house blow away?" I ask.

"Don't worry, honey," says Mommy. "Houses are tough. This house has been through lots of hurricanes before."

The wind grows wild. The trees bend right over and touch the ground. Branches crack and snap.

"This is it," Daddy says.

It sounds like a railroad train is roaring right by our house. The windows shake in their frames.

Pepper buries his nose in my lap. I close my eyes and hug him tight.

Then, suddenly, it is quiet. I open my eyes. The sun is shining.

"This is the eye of the hurricane," Daddy says. "It lasts only a few minutes."

Mommy and Daddy and I step outside. It's strangely still, as if the whole world has stopped and nothing is alive anywhere.

Then dark clouds cover the sun and the wind comes tearing back across the meadow. We dart back inside the house just in time.

All the lights go out.

"A tree must have fallen across the power lines," Mommy says.

It's too dark to work on the puzzle, so Daddy gets out his harmonica.
He plays all my favorite songs, even the ones I used to like when I was real little.

Slowly, the wind quiets down. The weather radio tells us that Hurricane Bob
has passed us now.

"Whew!" I say, but I feel a little sad, too, like when the circus left town.

The electric stove doesn't work, so we make a salad from the vegetables I
picked. We eat dinner by candlelight.

We all go to bed early. Mommy reads me my goodnight story while I hold the flashlight. Pepper curls up on my bed. He is asleep before the story is over.

In the morning I run outside. Some trees have been broken off at the waist; some have their roots in the air. There are branches everywhere and our garbage can is upside down in a bayberry bush. The tomato plants in the garden are withered and black. The peas I planted have been ripped from the trellis.

In the meadow, the long grasses have been flattened, as if a giant had been stomping around. But the birds are calling. A rabbit is nibbling on the leaves of a tree that got knocked down. There are hoof prints along the dirt road, so I know the deer are okay, too.

"What about *Allegro*?" I ask Daddy.

"Let's go check on her," he says.

We all drive down to the bay. People are out with chain saws, cutting up fallen trees. It sounds like a new town is being built.

At the harbor, some sailboats are bobbing upside down. Lots of boats have blown up on shore. I run to see *Allegro*. She is safe at the dock.

We go for a walk along the beach. Mussels and scallops have been washed up high with the tide. I see a dead herring gull lying against the dunes.

When we go home the power is still out. We have no running water. The stove doesn't work, and the toilet can't flush. It's like living in the olden days. We cook on an outdoor fire, and rinse off in a pond. At night there are no outside lights and the stars seem very bright. I think maybe it will be this way forever.

Two days go by, then three, then four. The leaves turn brown and some trees are bare. It's August still, but it looks like November.

On the fifth night, just as we are starting dinner: magic! Our lights suddenly go on.

"The power's back!" says Mommy.

The refrigerator starts humming. The second hand on the clock starts sweeping around to make up for lost time.

We decide we still like to eat dinner by candlelight. And even though Hurricane Bob is nothing but a little breeze now, far away, Pepper still likes to sleep right on my bed.

Author's Note

Hurricanes are storms that have winds greater than 74 mph. They form in the Tropics, where there are two things they need to get going: warm water and converging air. A hurricane is called a "typhoon" in the western Pacific, or a "cyclone" in the Indian Ocean.

Hurricanes are strongest over water and lose their power once they hit land. They can make big waves in the ocean, even in places far away. The Weather Service grades a hurricane on a scale from one to five, according to the speed of its sustained winds. A category one hurricane, the weakest, has winds from 74 mph to 95 mph. A category five hurricane has winds 155 mph or above. Of course, with any hurricane there can be gusts of wind that are much stronger. Hurricane Bob was a category two hurricane.

Years ago, hurricanes were always given girls' names. Now they alternate girls' and boys' names. They start with the letter A for the first hurricane of the year, then run through the whole alphabet. But they don't have any hurricane names beginning with Q, U, X, Y, or Z. Hurricane Bob, which was in August of 1991, was the second one that year. The Weather Service has a six-year list of names for hurricanes, so they're all set for ones to come. If a hurricane has been especially severe, its name is retired for a long time.

The Weather Service uses satellite photographs to spot hurricanes forming, so they can give people plenty of warning. The storms start as tropical disturbances, then grow to tropical depressions, then tropical storms, then hurricanes. Barometers are instruments that measure air pressure. There's high pressure when the weather's good, low pressure when it's bad. When the barometer tells you air pressure is falling fast, watch out for a storm!